Tales of SILLINESS

Retold Timeless Classics

Perfection Learning®

Retold by Janice Kuharski

Editor:	Lisa Owens
Editorial Assistant:	Berit Thorkelson
Illustrator:	Michael A. Aspengren

For information, contact:
Perfection Learning® Corporation
1000 North Second Avenue, P.O. Box 500
Logan, Iowa 51546-1099
Phone: (800) 831-4190 • Fax: (712) 644-2392

Paperback ISBN 0-7891-2328-2
Cover Craft® ISBN 0-7807-7749-2
Printed in the U.S.A.

Contents

The Six Sillies

There once was a young girl who was very silly. Her parents were very silly too. Of course, none of them knew it.

One evening, the three sillies heard a loud knock at the door.

"Who can that be?" asked the mother.

"I don't know," answered the girl. "But they are knocking very loud. And very long."

"When someone knocks," said the girl's father, "it's a good idea to answer the door."

"How true!" replied the mother. "I should have thought of that myself!" And she sent the girl to answer the door.

Soon, the girl led a young man into the room. "This is Charles," she said. "He wishes to marry me!"

"Isn't that wonderful news?" cried the girl's happy mother.

"It certainly is!" agreed the girl's father. "News like this," he added, "calls for a party!"

The mother went to the kitchen to get a plate of cakes. And the girl went to the cellar. She was supposed to fetch a jug of cider from the wooden keg.

The mother returned with the cakes. But the girl did not return. The three people upstairs waited and waited.

At last, the girl's mother said, "I fear that something is wrong. I will go to the cellar and see for myself."

When the mother saw her daughter, she cried out in surprise. "Why are you sitting on the stairs?" she asked. "And why are you letting all the cider run out of the keg?"

"Oh, Mother! I have been thinking," the girl sobbed. "One day, I will have a child. And what shall I name him? I have thought and thought about it. But there are no names left. *Every* name I can think of already belongs to somebody else!"

Great tears rolled down the girl's cheeks. They fell on the cellar floor and mixed with the pool of cider.

"Hmm," said the mother, scratching her head. "That is a problem. But surely we are smart enough to solve it." And so the mother sat on the stairs and tried to think of new names.

Meanwhile, the father wondered what his wife and daughter were doing. He spoke to Charles. "Something must be wrong. I think I'll go to the cellar myself. Please make yourself comfortable. I'll be right back. Then we can have our party."

"My goodness!" exclaimed the father when he reached the cellar. "Why are you both sitting on the cellar steps? And why are you letting the cider run all over the cellar?" By now the cider had reached the middle steps.

"Can't you see that we are trying to think?" sobbed the mother.

"What are you thinking about?" asked the father.

"Our daughter will have a child one day. But what can she name him? For every name in the world already belongs to someone else. Our poor grandchild simply must have a name!"

"Hmm," replied the father, scratching his chin. "That is quite a problem. But there are three of us here. Three people thinking are always better than one—or two. So cheer up. We shall come up with a good name in no time!"

The three sillies sat on the steps. And they thought and thought. Upstairs, Charles waited and waited. But the family did not return.

Finally, Charles got worried. He said, "It does not take three people to get one jug of cider. There must be something terribly wrong." So Charles went downstairs to see for himself.

"What is this?" asked Charles. "Why are the three of you sitting and crying on the steps? And why is the cider running all over the cellar?" By this time, the cider had reached the top of the steps. The three sillies were sitting in it!

"Oh, it's just awful!" sobbed the father. "You see, one day you will have a child—will you not?"

"I hope so," answered Charles. "But why are you crying? That will be a happy occasion."

"My dear boy, you do not understand!" cried the father. "The baby will need a name. But there are no names left in the world. Every name we can think of already belongs to someone else. Don't you see? Your poor child will have to go through life without a name. And that is such a sad, sad thing!"

Charles couldn't believe his ears.

"Well," he began. "The answer is simple. It is true that every name already belongs to somebody else. But no one minds when you reuse a perfectly good name. It's done all the time. There, now. The problem is solved!"

"Indeed!" exclaimed the three sillies. "Why didn't we think of that?"

Charles watched as the silly family dried their tears and wrung cider from their clothes. He thought about his future for a moment. Then he said to the father, "I must leave now. I have decided to look for three people who are sillier than the three of you. If I find them, I will come back and marry your daughter.

"In the meantime, please close the tap on the keg," Charles added. "Who knows? There could be a wedding after all. Then we would certainly need whatever cider is left!"

Charles left the little house and walked a few miles down the road. He stopped to rest at an orchard. There he saw a strange sight. A man holding a long-handled fork was shaking walnuts from a tree. Then he used the fork to try to throw the walnuts into a cart. Most of the walnuts hit the ground. Very few landed in the cart.

"Good day to you, sir," Charles said to the man. "I see you are having a difficult time. How long have you been at your work?"

"I have been here since early morning."

"Here is what you should do," said Charles politely. "Get a very large basket. Collect the walnuts in it first. Then load them into the cart. Your work will be done before you know it!"

"What a good idea!" replied the man. "I will get a basket at once. I cannot thank you enough."

Charles continued on his way. He couldn't believe how easy it had been to find the first silly person.

In a little while, Charles stopped at a farmer's field. Here, too, he saw a strange sight. The farmer and his pig were standing next to a large tree. And the farmer was yelling at the pig.

"Go on now. Jump! Jump up the tree!" yelled the farmer to the pig. But the pig did not jump. He just gave a loud grunt and lay down.

"Excuse me, sir," said Charles. "Why do you yell at your pig?"

"I am trying to feed acorns to my pig," replied the farmer. "But he is very stubborn. He refuses to jump up the tree to get them."

"You know, pigs are not fond of climbing trees," said Charles. "So why not climb the tree yourself? If you shake the tree as hard as you can, the acorns will fall to the ground. And your pig will have a fine feast."

The farmer thanked Charles for his help. Then he said, "I only wish you had come by sooner. How much time I might have saved!"

Charles shook his head in disbelief. He had found the second silly person! He said, "Perhaps I will find a third fool just as quickly."

Just before nightfall, Charles stopped at a little cottage. Beside the cottage stood a tall tree. A pair of trousers was hanging from the tree. And next to the tree stood a man. Over and over, the man tried jumping into the legs of the trousers. But it didn't work. The trousers flapped in the wind. And the poor man stood shivering in his underwear.

"Dear sir," Charles began, "you must be getting very tired. How long have you been jumping?"

"Most of the day, lad," replied the man. "But soon enough, it will be bedtime. Then I won't need trousers at all."

"I think I can help," said Charles. "First, take the trousers from the tree. Then step into them carefully—one leg at a time. That is how I do it. And it works every time!"

"You are very kind," said the man. "And very clever as well!"

Charles knew that he had found the third and silliest fool of all. And he intended to keep his promise.

So Charles traveled back to the home of the three silly people. He asked for the girl's hand in marriage. And all three sillies answered with a very loud "YES!"

Charles and the girl married the very next morning. Why wait? And a year later, they had their first child. Fortunately, they had no trouble picking a name.

"Charles is a very good name," the couple agreed. They liked it extremely well. So well, in fact, that they used it again and again—for all six of their silly children!

BLOCKHEAD HANS

Once there was a very rich farmer. He lived in a great mansion with his three sons. The first two sons were said to be very clever. But the youngest son was rumored to be quite stupid.

One day, the king's daughter announced that she was looking for a husband. She said that the man she chose would be clever. And very good with words. The princess planned to hold a contest at the court. She herself would be the judge.

The two elder sons went to their father at once. Each one believed he was clever enough to win. But both needed a horse and money to get to the court.

The farmer spoke to his first son. "Dear son," he said, "I know how very clever you are. You know all the words there are to know. And you remember everything you have ever read. You stand a good chance of winning. Therefore, I will send you off on a fine black horse. With money to spare!"

Then the farmer spoke to his second son. "You also have a very good brain, my boy. You know all the laws of the land. And you make wonderful speeches. You stand a good chance of winning as well. So I will send you off with some money and my best white horse. Good luck to you both!"

The third son heard what his brothers were doing. And he went to his father.

"May I speak with you, Father?" said the third son. "I would like to go to the contest too. Maybe *I* could win the hand of the princess."

The first two sons jeered at their brother. "How ridiculous!" they cried. "You could never win anything by being clever!"

"The princess would laugh in your face!" said the first son.

"Have you forgotten what your name is?" taunted the second son. "No princess would marry someone named Blockhead Hans!"

The old farmer had to agree with his two clever sons. But Blockhead Hans still wished to enter the contest.

"Very well, Blockhead Hans," said the farmer. "You may go if you wish. I will give you the old nanny goat. But don't expect even a penny to carry along!"

"Thank you, Father," replied Blockhead Hans. "The old nanny goat will do well enough. Now I can travel with my brothers. Slap! Bang! I'm on my way. Maybe I'll win a princess today!"

Blockhead Hans's brothers did not wait for him. They galloped ahead on their fine horses. Poor Blockhead Hans was left behind in a cloud of dust.

In a short while, though, Blockhead Hans caught up with his brothers. He sang out as he approached them. "Heigh-ho! Heigh-ho! What do you know? Look! I've found an old black crow!"

Blockhead Hans held up the dead crow and waved it about.

"Blockhead has an old dead crow!" laughed the first son.

"Hey, Blockhead! What good is a vile thing like that?" sneered the second son.

"You will see," replied Blockhead Hans. "It is just what I need to win the princess."

The two elder brothers galloped ahead again. But soon, they heard a noise behind them. Blockhead Hans was singing at the top of his voice. "Heigh-ho! Heigh-ho! What do you say? I've found a lovely shoe today!"

Blockhead Hans's two brothers turned around. Blockhead Hans was holding an old wooden shoe.

"I suppose you're going to give that to the princess too!" scoffed the first son.

"Of course I am!" replied Blockhead Hans. "It's just the thing to win the princess's hand."

"Blockhead Hans is even crazier than I thought," said the second son. "Let's try to leave him behind."

But Blockhead Hans caught up with his brothers again. This time, he held something in both hands. He sang, "Heigh-ho! Heigh-ho! Just look at this. Here's some mud to win a lady's kiss!"

The first two sons burst out laughing. "Poor Blockhead Hans!" they said to each other. "He's gone completely mad. Mud will certainly never help him win a princess."

"This mud is grand," replied Blockhead Hans. "Good mud—from the king's own land." Then he poured the mud into his pocket.

Finally, the three men reached the palace gate. There was a huge crowd. Hundreds of men were there to see the princess. Palace guards crowded everyone into a great hall. One by one, each man was called forward. Each one tried to show his cleverness with words. And each one forgot every word he planned to say.

The princess just laughed. "Throw him out!" she cried. "Away with him!" she ordered. "They are such fools! Now who's next?"

It was the first son's turn. He bowed to the princess. When he opened his mouth to speak, nothing came out!

"Speak louder," said the princess. "I cannot hear you. And neither can the reporters." She pointed to a group of people standing next to the window. They were furiously taking notes. They hoped to get a juicy story out of the contest.

The first son tried to speak again. "It's so hot in here," he muttered.

"Of course it is!" answered the princess. "My father is roasting young chickens today. Now let me hear your speech."

"I . . . uh . . . ahem!" was all that came out of his mouth. The reporters wrote it down anyway.

"Take him away at once," demanded the princess.

Now it was the second son's turn. He knew exactly what he wanted to say to the princess. He had practiced it many times. He bowed to the princess and opened his mouth to speak.

"I . . . uh . . . how do you do?" mumbled the second son.

"I can't hear a word you're saying!" yelled the princess. "Speak up!"

He tried to speak again. "I . . . um . . . it's so. . . so hot in here," he gasped.

"Yes, it is hot," answered the princess. "We are roasting young chickens today. If you have nothing more to say, leave at once!"

The second son joined his older brother.

And so Blockhead Hans came forward. He was riding his father's old nanny goat.

"I say, princess!" exclaimed Blockhead Hans. "It is roasting hot in here!"

"That's because we are roasting young chickens today!" answered the princess.

"Slap! Bang!" replied Blockhead Hans. "A nice hot fire is a very fine thing. It's just right for the meaty crow I bring!"

Blockhead Hans held out the crow for the princess to see.

"He is meaty indeed," replied the princess. "But what will you roast him in?"

"Look here, dear lady!" cried Blockhead Hans. "How lucky for you! I've brought along this lovely shoe."

Hans held out the old broken shoe. The princess studied it.

"That will do nicely," said the princess. She took the shoe and put the crow inside. Then she set it over the fire to cook. Then she said, "I always like a good strong broth to go with a meal," she said.

As if on cue, Blockhead Hans scooped some of the mud from his pocket. He held it out for the princess to see.

"Don't worry, my dear!" cried Blockhead Hans. "Just look at this. I'll trade this good strong broth for a kiss!"

The princess blushed. She kissed Blockhead Hans on the cheek.

"You're a clever lad," she said. "And you are very good with words. I have no choice but to marry you! What is your name?"

Blockhead Hans bowed to the princess. He worried that his name would disappoint her. He searched her face for a long moment. "My name is Blockhead Hans," he said at last.

"How can that be?" asked the princess. "You are far too clever for such a name. It does not suit you at all."

Suddenly, Blockhead Hans's eldest brother stepped forward. "Pardon me, milady," he said. "But this man has always been a blockhead. Since the day he was born."

"That's right," agreed the other brother. "We are his brothers. We see him every day. So we know how dumb he is. I beg of you—think of your country. If you marry this oaf, you will disgrace the king, yourself, and your people."

The princess listened carefully to the brothers. They told tale after tale about Blockhead Hans. They wanted to prove how stupid their younger brother really was.

Meanwhile, the reporters wrote everything. They couldn't wait to share this story with the rest of the land. Imagine! Their beloved princess had chosen a blockhead as her bridegroom. What a scandal!

Finally, the princess had heard enough. "Silence!" she shouted.

A hush fell over the crowd. And the princess motioned for Blockhead Hans to stand near her. He swiftly went to her side.

"This man passed every
remarked the princess. "K
other man here failed. If this
one more task to my satisfa
paused to look at the brothers, th
then the rest of the crowd. "If he do
marry him. For it will prove him to be

Hans replied sincerely, "I'll do anything for
you, fair lady. All you have to do is ask."

The princess stepped closer to Blockhead
Hans. Then she whispered to him, "Look over
there. Do you see the reporter with the gray
hair? He writes such mean and untrue things
about me. Defend my honor, and I shall be
yours forever."

With a smile, Blockhead Hans reached into
his pocket. He said, "Slap! Bang! This is more
than just a whim. I'll sling this lovely mud. And
aim it right at him!"

The mud sailed across the room and hit the
old reporter right in the eye!

"Well done, Hans!" exclaimed the happy
princess. "We shall get along very well."

And they did indeed.

Lazy Jack

There was a young girl who lived in a fine stone house. She had everything she needed. And yet she never laughed. She didn't even smile. Everyone tried to cheer her. Her mother tried. Her father tried. All the servants tried. Until finally, they all stopped. "What is the use?" they asked. "She will neither smile nor laugh. And that is that!"

Meanwhile, a boy named Jack lived miles away in another part of town. Jack and his mother lived in a tiny cottage near a stream. Jack's mother worked all day long. She earned money by spinning. But it was never enough.

You see, Jack was a growing boy. His appetite was growing too. He ate and ate and ate and ate. And when he wasn't eating, he was napping. Between eating and napping, he had no time left for work. That, at least, is what Jack told his mother.

One day, Jack's mother called for him. She said, "The neighbors are calling you 'Lazy Jack.' You eat and sleep all day long. And you never do a lick of work. I am running out of patience, Jack. I am also running out of bread and porridge. So from now on, you must earn your keep."

"But how can I, Mother?" asked Jack. He was chewing on some bread and butter. "I've never worked before. All I know how to do is eat and sleep. Who would hire a boy like me?" Jack finished the bread and drank the rest of his milk.

"The farmer would!" exclaimed Jack's mother. "He needs a helper today. He will pay you a penny for your work. Now hurry along. The roosters are already up. And so are the hens, the cows, and the goats!"

So Jack went off to work for the farmer. At the end of the day, the farmer gave Jack a penny.

"Thank you," said Jack. "I will carry this home to my mother."

But Jack did not go straight home. He was very tired from working all day.

"I think a swim in the stream is just what I need," said Jack.

Jack wondered what to do with the penny. "I know," he said. "I will balance it on my nose." But as soon as he started swimming, the penny fell off his nose and into the stream.

When Jack got home, his mother greeted him happily. "We can use your wages to buy a fine dinner. We'll eat sausages and eggs with our bread tonight."

"We could," said Jack, "if I had the penny. But I'm afraid it fell into the stream when I went swimming."

"How did it fall into the stream?" asked Jack's mother.

"Well, I balanced the penny on my nose. But as soon as I went underwater, it fell off."

"Silly boy!" exclaimed Jack's mother. "That is no way to carry a penny. You must carry it in your pocket. Remember that when you work for the dairyman tomorrow."

"Of course!" said Jack. "That's what I'll do the next time."

The next morning, Jack ate his breakfast and went off to the dairy farm. He milked the cows. He carried the pails. He poured the milk into jars. The work kept Jack very busy. He didn't have time for even one short nap. At the end of the day, Jack had earned a jar of fresh milk.

"Thank you," Jack said to the dairyman. Remembering his mother's words, he carefully put the jar into his pocket.

"Good for me," Jack said to himself. "Now the milk will be safe until I get home."

But Jack was wrong. As he walked, the milk slopped and dripped all over the ground. When Jack got home, the milk was all gone.

Once again, Jack's mother greeted him warmly.

"I hope that the dairyman has paid you in milk," she said. "I have just made a cake. And what is better with cake than a glass of fresh milk?"

"Nothing," replied Jack. "But the milk is gone."

"Did you drink it on the way?" his mother asked.

"I did not," said Jack. "It all spilled from the jar I carried in my pocket."

"Silly boy!" exclaimed Jack's mother. "You should have carried the jar on top of your head. That is the way to carry milk, son."

"Yes, you are right," Jack told his mother. "That's what I'll do next time."

The next morning, Jack's mother woke him up. Jack yawned. It was too early to be up. But his mother said, "Eat your porridge quickly, Jack. You have another job this morning. The dairyman's brother needs some help today."

So Jack went off to work for the dairyman's brother. He did not milk the cows that day. Instead, he helped make the cheese. It was very good cheese. Jack ate some of it for lunch. Then the dairyman's brother gave him a big piece of cheese to take home for dinner.

"Remember, Jack," said the man. "You must keep this out of the sun."

"I have just the place for it," said Jack. And he put the big piece of cheese on top of his head. He covered it with his hat.

When he got home, Jack said proudly, "Mother! I have brought home a very nice piece of cheese. Now we can have bread and cheese for our dinner tonight."

"We could," said Jack's mother. "But you are wearing melted cheese on your hair, your face, and your hat. You must *always* carry cheese in your hands, Jack. You really should have known better."

"How true!" exclaimed Jack. "I'll be sure to do that the next time."

Early the next morning, Jack went off to work for the baker. Jack cracked the eggs. He measured the flour. He mixed the dough and put it into pans to bake. Jack thought he would get a cake or pie for lunch. But all he got was some stale bread.

"Surely, I will get something much better at the end of the day," said Jack.

But the baker was a very stingy man. He gave Jack a big gray tomcat—and nothing else!

"Oh, well," sighed Jack. "At least a cat is good for keeping the mice away."

Then Jack remembered his mother's words. He carefully picked up the cat. He tried to carry it in his hands. But that was a big mistake. The cat scratched, bit, and jumped out of his hands.

"My goodness!" cried Jack's mother when she saw him. "What a fight that cat put up! But I'll tell you why it happened. A cat is a funny animal. You need to show him who's in charge.

Tie him with a string. And then pull him along behind you."

"You're right," said Jack. "I will do that the next time."

The next day, Jack's mother woke him up early again. "Today," she said, "the butcher needs a helper. Let's hope he's not as stingy as the baker. Maybe he'll give you some good meat for our dinner tonight."

So Jack went off to help the butcher. All morning, he helped the butcher cut meat. He hung the meat on hooks. It was very hard work. But the butcher liked Jack's work. He paid Jack with a very large ham.

"I know what to do with this," said Jack. "I must tie it to a string."

And that is what he did. All the way home, Jack pulled the ham behind him. But Jack could not keep the barking dogs away. They followed Jack's ham on a string. They barked, yipped, and howled. As Jack walked along, more and more dogs joined the pack. What a noise they made! And what a time they had eating Jack's ham on a string!

When Jack got home, his mother was cooking eggs. "I hope," she said, "that we have ham or bacon to eat with our eggs tonight."

"Well, Mother," replied Jack, "I'm afraid not. You see, all the way home, dogs followed my ham on a string." Jack held up the string. "And now," Jack said, "there is nothing left but the bone."

"Oh, my silly, silly Jack!" his mother exclaimed. "I thought everyone knew how to carry a ham."

"How, Mother?" asked Jack.

"Very simple," she replied. "A large ham should be carried on your shoulder. Then the dogs will not smell it. And they will not follow you."

"Certainly, Mother!" said Jack. "I'll do it the very next time!"

The next day was Saturday. Jack stayed home to help his mother. He cleaned the cottage from top to bottom. His mother did more spinning. On Sunday, Jack finally got to rest. He ate a big bowl of porridge for breakfast and another for lunch. Then he slept the rest of the day. He did not even wake up for dinner!

On Monday, Jack's mother shook him. "Wake up, Jack," she said.

Jack got up and rubbed the sleep from his eyes. "Where am I going today?" he asked.

"Today, you will work for a man who herds donkeys," she said. "Now hurry off. He does not need a lazy worker. His donkeys are lazy enough!"

All day long, Jack worked for the donkey herder. "Giddyap. Giddyap!" Jack shouted at the donkeys.

But the donkeys just looked at him. "Hee-haw! Hee-haw!" they brayed. That meant, "We will go when we are ready—and not a second sooner."

Little by little, Jack moved the donkeys down the path. At the end of the day, Jack was very, very tired.

"You are a fine young fellow, Jack," said the donkey herder. "You seem to have a way with these donkeys of mine. So I am giving you one of them for your wages. I hope you know what to do with him," said the man.

"I certainly do!" replied Jack. And without another word, Jack picked up the donkey. He slung him across both shoulders and started to walk home.

"This is not bad at all," said Jack. "This time, I know what I'm doing!"

The donkey did not agree. "Hee-haw! Hee-haw!" brayed the donkey. Then he began to twist, wiggle, and squirm. He brayed even louder. "Hee-haw! Hee-haw! Hee-haw!" the donkey cried. Soon folks came out of their shops and houses to see what was happening.

"Look!" said the farmer. "It's Lazy Jack!"

The dairyman and his brother came out. "It's a fool with a donkey!" they cried.

The baker and the butcher came outside too. "Look at that!" they cried. "Lazy Jack has a donkey on his back!"

Everyone began to laugh. "HA! HA! HA! HO! HO! HO!" They laughed so hard that their stomachs shook. And tears rolled down their cheeks. More and more people came out to see the strange sight. One of them was the girl who lived in the fine stone house. It was the girl who neither laughed nor smiled. She could not believe her eyes.

First, the corners of her mouth turned up. Next, she began to smile. A moment later, she started to chuckle. Then her chuckle became a laugh. "HA! HA! HA! HO! HO! HO!" she laughed. And she kept right on laughing. She couldn't stop!

The girl's parents came outside to see why everyone was laughing. They stared in disbelief. For here were two amazing sights.

Lazy Jack with a braying donkey on his shoulders! And a daughter who was laughing with glee!

"How wonderful!" they cried. "Lazy Jack has done what no one else could ever do. He has made our daughter laugh. And now that she is happy, she is the prettiest girl in town."

Jack thought so too. He asked the girl in the fine stone house to marry him.

"Yes!" said the girl without blinking an eye. She smiled from ear to ear.

The girl's parents agreed to the match. "Jack makes her happy," they said. "And that makes us happy too!"

As time went on, people forgot that Jack had ever been lazy. Now he had a wife, a mother, five children, and a fine stone house to take care of. And all of that kept him busy for the rest of his life!

The Emperor's New Clothes

Many years ago, there was an emperor who did not care much for ruling his kingdom. He spent little money on his soldiers. He spent even less on his subjects. All the king's money went for one thing, and one thing only. The finest clothes money could buy!

When the hour changed, the emperor changed his clothes. He wore new clothes at every party and every meeting. And he took long walks in the city just to show them off!

One day, the emperor was dressing for a meeting. He had a fine new silk jacket to put on. His chief advisor came in with some exciting news.

"Excuse me, my lord," said the advisor. "I know you are busy. But there are two strangers outside who are asking to see you. They claim to be weavers. Weavers of the finest cloth in the world. Did you send for them, Your Majesty?"

The emperor frowned and stroked his chin for a moment. Then he said, "I do not remember asking for new weavers. But I will see them anyway. Send them in at once."

So the two strangers were invited inside. They told the emperor about the wonderful cloth they made. They said there was nothing like it in the entire world. And they said it was so special that not everyone could see it. Foolish people could not see it. And people unfit for their jobs could not see it. But wise people— like the emperor—could see it very well!

"This sounds like very special cloth indeed," said the emperor. "It's just what I need. No one else will have anything like it." So the emperor hired the strangers to weave the wonderful cloth. He provided them with a lovely room in the palace. They set up their weaving looms there. He also gave them money to buy the finest silk and gold thread. And then he waited to see the wonderful cloth.

Six weeks went by. The weavers worked constantly. The emperor could hardly wait to see his new cloth. But the cloth still wasn't ready. So he decided to peek inside the weaving room. Just then, he remembered what the weavers had said. They'd said that a fool would not be able to see the cloth.

"Of course, I have nothing to worry about," said the emperor to himself. "But to be safe, I will send in my chief advisor first. He will know how to judge the cloth. And I will find out if my chief advisor is truly clever—or just a fool."

The emperor's chief advisor entered the weaving room. The weavers were working away at their looms. They stopped their work and greeted the chief advisor. Then they pretended to hold up a piece of cloth. "Here is what we have done already," said the weavers, grinning. "How do you like it?"

The chief advisor blinked his eyes. He could not see a thing. Only the empty air.

Goodness, thought the chief advisor. I cannot let the emperor know about this. He will think I am a fool. And then I will lose my job.

The weavers again pretended to hold up the cloth. The chief advisor pretended to look very closely. "Why, this cloth is amazing!" he said.

"Such color! Such a nice design! It is truly the most beautiful cloth I have ever seen."

And that is exactly what the chief advisor told the emperor. The emperor was very pleased. And when the weavers asked for more money, he gave it to them gladly. For how could they finish the wonderful cloth if they ran out of silk and gold? The weavers thanked the emperor and kept the money for themselves.

Another week passed. But the cloth was still unfinished. This time, the emperor sent in a different advisor to check the weavers' work.

Now the second advisor went into the weaving room. The weavers stopped working. They pretended to hold up a corner of the cloth. "Is this not the most beautiful cloth you have ever seen?" they asked.

The advisor put on his spectacles. He pretended to look at the cloth. He cleared his throat. Then he said, "I—I am speechless. I have no words to describe it."

And that was true. For the poor advisor saw nothing but the empty air! Under his breath he said, "I cannot let the emperor know about this. It would prove that I am a fool. And then I would lose my job!"

"What do you think of the color?" asked one of the weavers.

"It—it is rich," answered the advisor. "A very deep, rich color!"

"And what about the design?" asked the other weaver.

"Most unusual," replied the advisor. "Truly one of a kind."

The emperor was very pleased to hear his advisor's report. But he could not wait any longer to see for himself. "Tomorrow," he said, "I will go to the weaving room. I will invite all the important people of the court to go as well. Everyone has been talking about my wonderful cloth. Now we shall see it at last."

The next day, the emperor and his court entered the weaving room. The weavers smiled and bowed. "Your Majesty," they said, "we hope you will be pleased. Here is the cloth. Come and see it for yourself."

The emperor looked at the looms. He looked at the weavers who were pretending to hold up the cloth. And he looked around the room. Nowhere did he see even the tiniest piece of cloth. The emperor opened his mouth to speak. But no words came out.

The chief advisor spoke up and addressed the group. "His Majesty is very, very pleased. The cloth is so beautiful that words escape him."

The emperor agreed. "You are quite right," he nodded. "How does one describe such a work of genius? I am so overwhelmed. I must get some air."

The emperor stepped out onto the balcony. To himself he said, "Fool! I must be the only one here who does not see the cloth. But I must pretend to see it. Otherwise, people will think that I am unfit to rule the land!"

With new determination, the emperor went back inside.

"Are you pleased with our work, my lord?" the weavers asked. They bowed politely again.

"Yes—of course I am!" exclaimed the emperor. "You've done excellent work! Who could disagree?"

Not one person disagreed. Everyone in the room said that the cloth was amazing. It was fit for an emperor. And everyone said that the weavers should make clothes from the cloth. Yes, new clothes for the emperor!

The chief advisor had an idea. "Why should we be the only ones to see the new clothes?" he asked. "Let's have a great procession. That way, the whole town can see the emperor's wonderful clothes."

And that is just what happened. The weavers worked in the weaving room for a week. They took the cloth from the loom. They cut it with huge scissors. They sewed the pieces with needles and thread. And finally they said, "His Majesty's clothes are finished."

The emperor went to the weaving room. The weavers held out a new coat for the emperor. And new trousers too.

"Feel the cloth, Your Majesty!" said the weavers. "It's as light as air. Don't you agree?"

"Oh, yes!" exclaimed the emperor. And he allowed the weavers to help him into the clothes. "Why, this is like wearing nothing at all!" he cried.

The emperor went over to the looking glass. He turned this way and that. He strutted back and forth. And he acted pleased with what he saw.

"These clothes have a wonderful fit," said the emperor as he sat down. "And the colors! I cannot wait to show them to my subjects!" he exclaimed.

At that moment, the emperor's chief advisor came in. He said, "They are waiting for you outside, Your Majesty. The procession will begin as soon as you are ready."

"Why, I am ready now!" replied the emperor. "Send in the servants to help me to the courtyard."

The servants promptly entered the room. At the emperor's urging, they pretended to hold up the train of his long coat. It would not do to let the coat touch the ground. Then the emperor walked proudly out to the courtyard. The members of the court followed.

The streets were lined with people. They were all eager to see the emperor. They'd heard many rumors about his new finery.

As the procession traveled down the street, a whisper flew through the crowd. It grew louder and louder.

"Look! Look at the emperor's new clothes!" the townspeople cried. "Such colors! Such a fine material! And such a wonderful fit!" they cried.

A loud cheer filled the air. "Hip hip hooray! Hip hip hooray!"

At the end of the procession, the emperor gave a speech. He thanked the weavers for their fantastic work. Then he declared, "I hereby appoint you to posts of great honor. You shall be the official weavers of the emperor's court."

The weavers smiled. They bowed to the king. Then they bowed to the great crowd. Another loud cheer rang out. For a while, everyone's eyes were fixed on the weavers and the happy, smiling emperor.

Without warning, a small child broke free from his mother. He ran toward the emperor. He reached up to touch the emperor's coat. Then he ran back to his mother.

"Mother!" cried the boy. "It's like I thought. The emperor's not wearing a coat. He's not wearing trousers either."

"Hush," said the boy's mother. "You're too young to know better."

The little boy spoke again. "But Mother!" he cried. "Can't you see? The emperor has no clothes!"

This time, the people in the crowd heard the boy. And they became very quiet.

After a moment of stunned silence, the crowd started buzzing.

"Did you hear what he said?" they asked each other. One by one, people repeated the boy's words. "It's true!" they exclaimed. "The little boy is right. The emperor has no clothes!"

It wasn't long before the emperor heard what the crowd was saying. The members of the court heard it too. And they also began to whisper, "The emperor has no clothes!"

The emperor looked down at his trousers. But he wore none! Then he looked at his long coat. But no coat was there!

"The boy is right," said the emperor to himself. "I have been a very great fool indeed!"

The emperor considered the situation. Then he said, "I am still the emperor after all. And people must not think that their emperor is a fool."

So the emperor pretended to straighten his clothes. He stood very tall and very proud. He took a step forward. The servants picked up the train of the emperor's coat. And the great procession went back to the emperor's palace.

The Play

The Emperor's New Clothes

Cast of Characters

Narrator
The Emperor
Li Ping
Weaver One
Weaver Two
Chang Kwan
Servant
Wu Feng
Small Boy
Small Boy's Mother

Setting: The emperor's palace

Act One

Narrator: Chang Kwan bustled about the servant's quarters. He was putting finishing touches on the emperor's new jacket. There was to be a royal banquet at the palace later that night. So, of course, the emperor needed a new jacket. He would never think of wearing the same thing twice. And that kept Chang Kwan busy all day long. The emperor needed fresh clothes in the morning. Clothes for going out. Clothes for coming back. And different clothes for dinner or a banquet.

As soon as he finished, Chang Kwan hurried off to the emperor's dressing room. Li Ping was talking with the emperor about the evening's festivities. The emperor tried on the jacket and sent Chang Kwan away.

Emperor: This new coat fits me perfectly. I will be the envy of everyone at the banquet. Well, Li Ping, what do you think of my new coat?

Li Ping: It's a fine coat, Your Majesty. Your tailors have done an excellent job.

Emperor: And how are things coming along for the banquet, Li Ping?

Li Ping: Everything is nearly ready. But there is a slight problem in the courtyard. Two strangers—weavers—claim that you sent for them. I told them that there must be some mistake. As your chief advisor, I would know if you had sent for new weavers. You already have the finest weavers in the world.

Emperor: And what did they say to that?

Li Ping: They said that I must be mistaken. They insist that you sent for them. So I told them to wait while I spoke with you. What shall I tell them?

Emperor: Hmmm. I am quite happy with my own weavers. Still, I have heard that there are some fine weavers in distant cities. Perhaps I should see them after all. Send them in, Li Ping. But make it clear that I have only a few minutes to give them.

Li Ping: Whatever you say, Your Majesty. I will send them in at once.

Narrator: Li Ping showed the weavers to a private parlor. The weavers bowed as the emperor entered the room.

Weaver One: Your Majesty. It is an honor to meet you. We have heard of your wonderful taste in clothing.

Weaver Two: And that is why we have come. We wish to offer our services.

Weaver One: Exactly! We are weavers of the finest cloth in the world.

Weaver Two: And nothing would please us more than to weave for you.

Emperor: I have many fine weavers already. They weave all sorts of rich and beautiful designs for me. Tell me. What is so special about the cloth you weave?

Weaver One: It is amazing cloth!

Weaver Two: Magical cloth!

Emperor: Magical? In what way?

Weaver One: It is magical because not everyone can see it.

Emperor: Now that sounds like a waste of my money! Why would I want such cloth?

Weaver Two: Oh, but you could see it very well, Your Majesty. And so could your advisors. Most of them, at least.

Emperor: Who cannot see this cloth?

Weaver One: Foolish people. People who don't do their jobs. Unworthy people cannot see the cloth. But everyone else can see it and admire it!

Emperor: That could be very useful. How much would I have to pay for this cloth?

Weaver One: Why, nothing, Your Majesty. Nothing at all.

Emperor: And how can you make this magical cloth for nothing?

Weaver Two: It is simple. We would charge nothing for the cloth itself. But naturally, we would need money to buy the supplies. Some strong silk thread. Some fine gold thread.

Weaver One: And weaving looms. Of course, we would need a room. A room in which to do our work. That's all we'd need. Then we can make you the most beautiful cloth you have ever seen!

Emperor: Reasonable. Very reasonable. Yes! Make the cloth! Weave for me this wonderful, magical cloth!

Weaver Two: When shall we start?

Emperor: Begin at once! By tomorrow morning, you shall have a room filled with all the supplies you need.

Weaver Two: Thank you, Your Majesty.

Weaver One: We cannot wait to begin!

Act Two

Narrator: Two weeks passed. No one had seen the weavers' new cloth. Not even the emperor. Chang Kwan gossiped with another servant outside the weaving room. The weavers usually kept the door shut. But today, the door was open a crack.

Chang Kwan: Shh! Let's try to get a peek inside the weaving room. I heard that the emperor is sending Li Ping in to take a look.

Servant: Why doesn't he go himself?

Chang Kwan: I think I know the reason. The emperor wants to find out if Li Ping is as clever as everyone thinks.

Servant: How will sending him to see the cloth show that?

Chang Kwan: Remember, the weavers say that a fool cannot see the cloth. Wait, Li Ping is coming! We'd better leave before he sees us!

Narrator: Chang Kwan and the other servant scurried from the scene. Li Ping entered the weaving room unannounced.

Li Ping: Good morning, gentlemen! I am Li Ping, chief advisor to the emperor. His Majesty has sent me to look at the cloth. I promised to give him a full report.

Weaver One: Ah, good sir. What perfect timing!

Weaver Two: We just finished a large piece of the cloth. Just look for yourself.

Li Ping: I'm ready, gentlemen. Where are you keeping the cloth?

Weaver One: Why, it is here, sir. Right in front of you. What do you think of the color? Have you ever seen anything like it?

Narrator: Li Ping could not see a thing! Was he a fool after all? Li Ping was afraid that the emperor would fire him. So he pretended to see the cloth.

Li Ping: The—the color is very deep and very rich. And the design—the design is very, very . . .

Weaver Two: Beautiful, isn't it? It is the best work we've ever done!

Weaver One: Do you think the emperor will be pleased? For that is what really matters.

Li Ping: Oh, yes. He will be pleased. There is nothing like it in the whole world.

Weaver Two: Thank you, kind sir. Visit again—whenever you wish!

Narrator: Li Ping wished that the emperor had sent someone else to see the cloth. What could he tell him? Then it hit him. Li Ping knew exactly what he would say to the emperor. He would tell him that the cloth was simply too beautiful. Too beautiful for words!

Act Three

Narrator: Two more weeks passed by. Wu Feng, another advisor, was in the weaving room. The emperor wanted to find out if Wu Feng was as clever as Li Ping. Once again, Chang Kwan stood outside the room. But this time, he was supposed to be there. He was waiting for Wu Feng's report on the cloth. You see, Wu Feng used a cane and walked very slowly. So Chang Kwan was to act as messenger. Soon, Wu Feng came out of the room.

Wu Feng: Ah, Chang Kwan! You are already here.

Chang Kwan: Yes, sir. The emperor wishes to know everything about his wonderful cloth. Tell me every detail. I have a good memory.

Wu Feng: But it would be impossible to tell you everything.

Chang Kwan: And why is that, sir?

Wu Feng: There is so much to tell. I cannot tell you everything at once. To begin with, the color is quite, quite . . .

Chang Kwan: Different?

Wu Feng: That is it, exactly. It is different. Different from any color I have ever seen. And the design is also very, very . . . What is the word?

Chang Kwan: Different?

Wu Feng: Yes! That is the very word to describe it!

Chang Kwan: What else shall I put in my report, sir?

Wu Feng: Say that no one in the world has cloth that is so—so—

Chang Kwan: Beautiful and different?

Wu Feng: Exactly. But I cannot say another word. For the emperor's cloth has left me speechless.

Narrator: With that, Chang Kwan hurried to the emperor's side. On the way, he talked to himself.

Chang Kwan: This cloth must be remarkable indeed. Either that or the emperor's top advisors are fools!

Act Four

Narrator: Two weeks later, the emperor sat in a special seat in the weaving room. Li Ping, Wu Feng, and other members of the court stood around him. At the other end of the room stood the weavers. They were next to the loom, which was covered with a sheet.

Weaver One: Welcome, Your Majesty.

Weaver Two: And welcome, members of the court. We are happy to unveil our work today.

Weaver One: We are sorry that it took so long. But we wanted everything to be just right.

Weaver Two: That's true. If we had worked too quickly or cheaply, the cloth would not be perfect. And that would disappoint His Majesty.

Emperor: Now get on with it, gentlemen. I have waited a long time. And I have spent a great deal of money. Show me the cloth.

Narrator: With one grand movement, the weavers removed the sheet from the loom. The emperor gasped. For he could not see the splendid cloth.

Weaver Two: What do you think, Your Majesty?

Emperor: I—I think you must hold it up by one end. That way I can get a better look at it.

Weaver One: Of course, Your Majesty. It is such a very large piece. It is hard for the eyes to see all of it at once.

Emperor: Yes! That's it exactly. It—it is too much to take in all at once.

Narrator: The emperor was beside himself. He saw nothing but the empty air. Yet he could tell no one. His people could not know that he was too foolish to see the cloth. So the emperor played along.

Emperor: No words can describe something as wonderful as this. Isn't that correct, Li Ping?

Li Ping: Oh, yes, Your Majesty. You are quite right.

Wu Feng: I, too, was speechless at first, Your Majesty. There was too much beauty to take in. Then I gave my eyes a chance to focus. And I saw all the wonderful details in the design.

Li Ping: And the rich shadings of color. It is truly amazing cloth. And worth every penny.

Emperor: Oh, yes! Worth every last penny. Worth every strand of silk and gold!

Li Ping: Indeed! The weavers must make His Majesty a fine new set of clothes!

Wu Feng: That is an excellent idea. And I have an even better idea.

Emperor: Let's hear it.

Wu Feng: Your subjects have been talking about the wonderful cloth for weeks. We should plan a great procession. Then the townspeople can see the emperor's new clothes for themselves.

Emperor: I like it. It is decided. When the new clothes are finished, we will have a great procession. And everyone will applaud the work of the most skilled weavers in the world!

<u>Act Five</u>

Narrator: The day of the great procession arrived. The emperor stood in front of a looking glass. And the weavers stood next to the emperor, one on each side. The weavers admired the emperor's new set of clothes. But the emperor felt foolish. All he saw was his underwear. Yet he was determined not to reveal himself as a fool.

Weaver One: What about the sleeves? Are they even?

Weaver Two: Oh, yes. They are the exact same length. Now, Your Majesty, how do your new clothes feel?

Emperor: They feel very light.

Weaver One: And how do they feel when you sit?

Emperor: They are comfortable. Very comfortable. These clothes are as light as air. It is like I am wearing nothing at all!

Narrator: Li Ping entered the emperor's dressing room.

Li Ping: When His Majesty is ready, we can begin the procession. The others are waiting in the courtyard.

Weaver One: Why, the emperor is ready now. Can't you see? He is wearing his brand-new clothes. They fit him well. Don't you think?

Li Ping: I have never seen a better fit. They fit him like—like his very own skin!

Weaver Two: Perhaps Chang Kwan could help us carry the train of this coat. It is quite a long train, isn't it, Chang Kwan?

Narrator: It was Chang Kwan's turn to be shocked. He could not see the train! But he knew what would happen if he admitted it. So he said what he knew he must.

Chang Kwan: I have never seen another train like it. You must show me how to carry it.

Weaver One: Here, Chang Kwan. Take this end of it. Be careful not to let it drop.

Chang Kwan: For such a long train, it is surprisingly light. And so easy to carry.

Li Ping: Your Majesty, we are all ready now. Shall we move to the courtyard?

Emperor: Yes, Li Ping. And let the procession begin!

Narrator: The crowd waved and shouted as the emperor came into view. They were eager to see the famed cloth.

Chang Kwan: How excited the townspeople are! Some of them are pressing forward to get a better look. What should we do?

Wu Feng: Tell the emperor's soldiers to keep the crowd back. We need more room to get through.

Chang Kwan: Look over there! That small boy is trying to get near the emperor. But he can't push through the crowd.

Narrator: The boy headed back toward his mother.

Small Boy: It is the emperor himself, Mother. Oh, how I want to see him up close.

Small Boy's Mother: Here, son. Climb onto my shoulders. Then you will be able to see better.

Narrator: The boy did as his mother said. He had a clear view of the emperor. And he was surprised by what he saw.

Small Boy: Look, Mother! The emperor has no coat. And no trousers. He has nothing on! Nothing but his underwear!

Small Boy's Mother: Hush, son! You are mistaken. Everyone can see what fine clothes the emperor is wearing.

Small Boy: But Mother. It's plain as day. The emperor is wearing no clothes!

Narrator: A hush fell over the crowd. They'd heard the small boy speak. And they couldn't believe their ears—or their eyes!

Li Ping: Did you hear what the little boy said? He said that the emperor's wearing no clothes!

Wu Feng: I heard it!

Li Ping: Is it true? Is the little boy right?

Narrator: The emperor bowed his head in shame. For deep down, he had known the truth all along. He spoke to Chang Kwan.

Emperor: The boy is right. What a great fool I have been!

Chang Kwan: Your Majesty! Where did the weavers go? I know I saw them a moment ago. Unless my eyes are fooling me again.

Emperor: No, Chang Kwan. You can believe your eyes this time. The weavers have disappeared into the crowd. And that is what I would like to do as well. But I have promised my subjects a great procession. And I shall not disappoint them. Are you still holding my coat, Chang Kwan?

Chang Kwan: Yes, Your Majesty.

Emperor: Then let us move forward. Remember, Chang Kwan, my coat has a very long train. It should not touch the ground.

Chang Kwan: Do not worry, Your Majesty. Not a speck of dust will touch it. Not one speck!

Narrator: With that, the great procession returned to the palace. And the emperor proudly led the way.